JUST PLAIN BOB

His Every FANTASY

HOT EROTICA

About the Publisher

4Fun Publishing, a member of **BLVNP Incorporated**, 340 S. Lemon #6200, Walnut CA 91789, info@blvnp.com / legal@blvnp.com

NOTE: Due to the highly emotional reaction of some people to works of erotic fiction, any email sent to the above address that contains foul language or religious references is automatically deleted by our anti-spam software and will not be seen. All other communications are welcome.

DISCLAIMER

His Every Fantasy
Hot Erotica

By: Just Plain Bob

© **Just Plain Bob 2014**
ISBN: 978-1-68030-060-4

Chapter 1

Everyone has fantasies. Some are sexual, some are financial and some are about fame. One guy's fantasy might be to be the quarterback that leads his team into the Super Bowl and another guy's might be to pitch the only really perfect game – 27 batters and 27 strike outs – in the World Series. I used to work with a guy whose fantasy was to find a lamp at an antique store, rub it and have a genie appear so he could wish for a ten-inch dick. And of course, everyone fantasizes about what they would do if they hit the 217 million dollar Power Ball lottery.

My fantasy was to be stranded on a deserted island with porn star Kristal Summers or be walking down a street and have a car pull over and a voice call out "Hey you!" I turn and see Kristal looking out the window smiling as she says, "I want you to be in my next video." Or a knock on my door some night and when I answer it I find Kristal standing there. "My car broke down in front of your place. Can you help me?" Or….oh well, you get the idea.

I found her one night while I was surfing porn sites on the Net and one look at that face and she had me. I have downloaded 11 videos of her and I am constantly looking for more. I spend more time on the computer than is good for me, but I don't have anything else to do. No, that isn't really true. There is a lot I could get out and do, but I have lost the desire to do any of it. If I left my computer and ventured out I would run into friends and friends being what they are they would try and cheer me up. Tell me that it was probably for the best and some would try to play matchmaker and fix me up with "this girl who is absolutely perfect for you."

And that is what I am afraid of. Another girl who is perfect for me. I've already had two girls who were "absolutely perfect for me" and between the two of them, they managed to rip my heart out.

The first one was Annalise. A five-foot, two-inch blond bombshell. At 36x23x34, she was a walking wet dream who stunned the hell out of me when she walked up to me at a party and said:

"The idiot who brought me to this party is a real drag. How about you take me out of here and we go find some place where we can have a few drinks, dance a little and get to know each other."

I might have been a little tongue-tied, but I wasn't stupid and I offered her my arm and we left the party. We went to the Starlight Lounge and drank, danced and talked and I found out that she was 24, a legal secretary, lived alone in an apartment on Sudsbury Avenue and that her favorite color was blue. She had no hometown loyalties; her favorite football team was the Cowboys, favorite baseball team was the Bluejays, the Red Wings were her hockey team and she had absolutely no interest in basketball.

"Those ugly tattoos they cover themselves with are absolutely disgusting."

She liked opera, ballet, classical music, bluegrass and hated 'rap' music. I wanted to ask her why she picked me, but I was afraid to. She might have said:

"I don't know, but now that we are here I don't think that it was such a good idea."

No sir! I didn't know why she picked me, but I was going to ride with it as far as it would go. I drove her home, asked for a date and she said yes. Three months later we were living together and a month after she moved in I proposed. The seven months we lived together before the wedding were glorious. Annalise was a good cook, fun to be with and a tiger in the bedroom.

The week before the wedding, I had a bachelor party and her girlfriends took her out for a bachelorette party. Mine was predictable. Some drinking, some card playing and about eleven o'clock a stripper arrived. She was fairly good looking and her dance and the lap dance that followed were okay, but didn't do a thing for me. Why would it? I had 'sex bomb' Annalise at home. I was asleep when Annalise got home and she was dead to the world when I got up to go to work in the morning.

Two days later, I received an envelope in the mail at work and when I opened it I found five things. A note that said "Are you sure that you want to marry this?" and four photos of Annalise being enjoyed sexually by at least six different men. In one picture she had a cock in her mouth, ass and pussy and in another she had her hand – left one with engagement ring showing – guiding a large cock into her mouth.

I took a personal day and left work and when Annalise got home from work that evening she found everything of hers boxed, bagged and waiting for her outside the front door. She still had a key though and when she came in I was sitting at the kitchen table sipping a beer and working a crossword puzzle. She didn't bother with a "Hi Honey" just asked me why her stuff was outside. I slid the envelope across the table to her and she opened it and looked at the contents and then at me.

"This doesn't mean anything honey. It was a last fling before I settled down into marriage. It has nothing to do with my love for you. It was just something that I wanted to try while I still could. There was no way that I would ever do it once I was married so I cut loose while I was still single. It is nothing, baby. Just a last hoorah before I take myself off the market."

"It might mean nothing to you Annalise, but someone who was at your orgy with you hates you enough to send me these pictures. That means they hate you enough to send them to God knows who. I will not go through the rest of my life having people look at me and say 'There goes that poor sucker who married that slut who does gangbangs.' I will not go through life watching guys who have seen those photos try and get you to sneak off with them and most of all, I will not go through life wondering if and when you might do it again."

"I would never do it again. I love you, baby and I know you love me."

"You're right, Annalise, I did love you and I probably will for a long time after you are gone, but I can tell from the expression on your face in these pictures how much you are loving it and I'll never be able to believe you won't want to do it again and I will not go through life waiting for that shoe to drop."

"I'm the best thing to ever happen to you Robert and you are going to throw me away over nothing?"

"I've already said it Annalise; it might mean nothing to you, but it means a hell of a lot to me. I'm sorry Annalise, but after seeing these pictures and seeing how much you seem to be enjoying it, I'll never be able to trust you not to do it again and I'll be damned if I'm going to spend my time checking up on you every time you have an unexplained absence or go out for a night out with the girls. We are history Annalise. Please go so I can start crying in my beer."

"Please Rob, don't make me go. I love you."

"Goodbye, Annalise."

She stared at me for several seconds and then she turned and left. I heard later that she quit her job and moved out of town.

~~***~~

I sulked for about six weeks and then friends being what they are, they began trying to cheer me up and the matchmaking began. I was introduced to some very nice and very lovely ladies and while I enjoyed the company of some and the beds of a few I never met one that had that 'spark' jump between us.

I went to a barbecue given by John and Marie Cochran and when I got there it 'just so happened' that there was a woman who had come alone and would I take her under my wing and see that she met everyone? She was a good looking lady and a pleasant company, but while I might date her a time or two, there was never going to be anything special and we both knew it. She had ridden to the party with a friend who had since left and I was asked to give her a ride home. I saw the hand of John and Marie in the whole set-up, but by then I was used to my friends trying to fix me up.

I drove Sue home and walked her to her door. I was surprised when she rang the bell and she told me that she had walked off and left her keys on the kitchen table.

"It's okay though. My roommate's car is in the parking lot so I know she is home and can let me in."

The door opened and I found myself looking into the eyes of Sue's roommate and my knees went weak. I've mentioned the lack of a 'spark' between me and some of the others my friends had fixed me up with, but there was a definite spark that jumped between Sue's roommate and me. I have no idea what the expression on my face looked like, but Sue looked from me to her roommate and then back at me and then said:

"Joan, this is Rob. Rob, this is my roommate, Joan and I'll just get out of the way and leave you two alone."

To shorten the story, I asked Joan out, she said yes and several months later I proposed and she said yes again.

~~***~~

Six years of what I thought was a perfect marriage came crashing down the day I came home from work early. They had shut the office down because of a gas leak scare in the building and had sent everybody home. Joan's car was at the drive, which I thought was odd since she didn't get off work until five. I knew as soon as I walked in the door what was going on. How could I not? The "Fuck me, oh God yes fuck me" was loud enough to be heard two blocks away. I walked up to the bedroom and saw a naked Joan with her legs up on the shoulders of Jake Winters who was Joan's supervisor at work. He was driving his cock into Joan and her hands were on his ass pulling him to her. Her eyes were closed and she was moaning "Fuck me, fuck me, fuck, me.'

My first instinct was to go in the room, pull him off Joan and stomp his balls into mush, but then I remembered what had happened to a guy I bowled with. He caught his wife on his bed with her lover and he ended up in jail charged assault. Since his wife had invited the man into the house and it was her house also, the man had every right to be in the house and my bowling buddy had no right to physically assault the man regardless of where in the house he had found him.

I didn't want jail in my future so I hurried downstairs and got the digital camera and the video camera and tri-pod. I quietly went back upstairs and set up the video camera in the hallway and focused it on the action on the bed. Then I went into the room. I got eight shots before they noticed me and then there was the mad scramble to separate. Jake was married and he knew he would be in deep shit if the pictures I'd taken ever got to his wife so he came after me to get the camera. He was so intent on getting the camera that he neglected to keep the family jewels protected and I drop kicked his nuts up into his throat. Then I kicked him a couple of times in the stones (if nine can be considered a 'couple') to make sure he stayed down. I grabbed him by the feet and dragged him downstairs and out the front door. I left him lying on the lawn and then I went back into the house and called 911.

I went back to the bedroom to confront Joan, but she is in the shower. I was sitting on the bed ignoring the doorbell, the knocks on the front door and the flashing red and blue lights coming through the bedroom window when Joan came into the room.

She looked at me, took a deep breath and said, "Sorry you had to see that."

"So am I. You mind telling me why?"

"Curiosity finally got the best of me."

"Care to explain that?"

"Let me get dressed first. You probably should go down and answer the door."

I opened the door to find two cops standing there and they wanted to know what happened and told them. They said I needed to go down to the station with them and I told them I be down a little later on, but at that moment I had some personal problems that I needed to address. One of them said:

"I'm afraid I must insist that you accompany us now."

"Insist away," I said, "I'll be there when I get there," and I closed the door in their faces and threw the deadbolt.

I went to the phone and called my boss, told him what had happened and asked if he could recommend a good lawyer and he gave me a name and a number. I called the guy, gave him the story and told him I would be going down to the station after I talked with my wife. He told me to call him just before I left the house and he would meet me at the station.

I went back to the bedroom and Joan was dressed and was packing a bag. "Okay," I said, "You're dressed. Do I get my explanation?"

"I told you. I was curious."

"About what?"

"His cock and how it would feel."

"You were curious about his cock?"

"For the last couple of years Jake has been trying to get in my pants and I've always kept him at arm's length. The girls in the office who had given in to him all gave him rave reviews. They said he had a huge cock and really knew how to use it and that I was missing the chance of a lifetime if I didn't give him a shot. Finally, curiosity got the best of me and I had to see for myself."

"From the sounds I heard when I walked in the front door it is obvious to me that you found the stories to be true."

"I'm sorry Rob, but it was the most amazing sexual experience of my life. His cock is just short of eleven inches and he touched me in places that I didn't even know I had."

"The most amazing sex of your life? You had to tell me that? Now I get to live the rest of my life knowing that I can't get the job done. Thanks a lot."

"I didn't mean it that way, honey. You always have gotten the job done. Jake was just different. It was all about cock size and what bigger would be like."

"How long has it been going on?"

"Today was the first time."

"And if I hadn't walked in on you, I'd have been getting sloppy seconds for the rest of my life and would have never known."

"No, you wouldn't. A little while longer for sure, but not the rest of your life. Jake usually only stays with one girl for three weeks or so and then he moves on to someone else."

"Then what? You go looking for your next big cock so you can have more amazing sexual experiences?"

"No I would not have. Jake satisfied my curiosity and after he moved on I would have gone back to being a faithful wife. I love you honey and I never expected you to find out. The last thing in the world that I wanted to happen was to lose your love. I thought I could have my little fling, satisfy my curiosity and then life would go back to normal and you would never have known."

"Well Joan, I hope it was worth your marriage because that is what it cost you."

"Of course it wasn't worth my marriage, Rob, but I can't undo what I have done. Water under the bridge I guess. Unless there is a chance you might be able to overlook my little mistake?"

"Sorry Joan. No way I could live with you and not remember what I saw on that bed every time I walked into this room."

"I'll be back this weekend to get the rest of my things." She picked up the suitcase and headed out of the room. She stopped at the doorway and turned. "I love you Rob. I really do and I'm sorry for this."

I heard her car start up and I went to the window and watched her drive away.

I went to the phone, called the lawyer, described myself to him and told him I was heading for the police station. As I turned the corner at the end of the block my rear view mirror showed four cop cars coming down the street and pulling up in front of the house. A bunch of cops spilled out and moved toward the house, some moving around to the back. I guess it must have upset them when I declined their invitation and closed the door in their faces.

I met Marvin Fastner in the parking lot at the police station and handed him the video camera and told him what was on it. He viewed the tape on the small viewing screen and smiled. I told him about the four cop cars at the house, but he didn't seem concerned.

The police were not happy with me. I kept my mouth shut and let Marvin handle it.

"My client' actions are totally understandable. Had he not remained in the house his wife could have used his absence to remove valuable property. In fact, she could have stripped the place bare. The officers did not arrest my client; they merely asked that he accompany them to the station and he was within his rights to decline their invitation."

The next item was what I had done to Mr. Winters. According to the police I had no right to do what I had done. It was a civil matter and should have been pursued through the courts. I had no right to physically attack Mr. Winters and I was going to be charged with assault and battery. Then Marvin played the video that showed Mr. Winters coming after me.

"My client was well within his rights to defend himself."

Then the cops brought up the fact, backed up by my own tape – that I had used excessive force after putting Mr. Winters down. At that point I spoke for the first time since entering the station.

"Get real here. Winters is six foot three and maybe two hundred and thirty pounds. I'm five ten and a hundred and seventy and only an idiot would take the chance of letting Winters get up and come after him. It was sheer assed good luck that I was able to put him down in the first place. Giving him a chance to get back at me would have been criminally stupid."

Then Marvin said, "If the government wants to waste its money taking this to trial we wouldn't mind at all giving a judge and jury a chance to have their say in the matter."

The matter was allowed to die quietly as far as the police were concerned.

~~***~~

The matter didn't die quietly as far as the other participants were concerned. Following Marvin's advice, I sued Winters for alienation of affections; I sued his employer for not enforcing the provisions in their company policy and procedures manual about relationships between supervisors and subordinates thus allowing Winters to have his way sexually with his female staff. My pictures found their way to Jake's wife and when the dust settled, Jake and Joan were unemployed, Jake was divorced and after Marvin took his cut, I was $212,609.42 richer and with an ex-wife.

The downside was that I did not trust women anymore so I stayed away from them. I was still needing sexual relief and the Net and my right hand took care of that need. It was while I was taking care of that need that I found Kristal Summers. For the next two or three months I played and replayed all of the downloads I'd made of her videos. Some of the sites not only had videos, but picture galleries and I printed off pictures of her and papered the walls of my den with them. And I fantasized and fantasized and fantasized.

One day as I was watching one of her videos, I was watching some guy fuck Kristal and I thought, "There is one lucky son of a bitch. He is actually getting paid to have sex with that Goddess." She was getting paid to have sex with him. She was getting paid to have sex with every man she had sex with in every film she made. I had over two hundred grand sitting in the bank so why didn't I use some of that money to see if I could get her to have sex with me? I would have to put some thought into it. I couldn't just go to her and say "How much to let me make love to you" because that would be illegal. It would be 'solicitation' on my part and if she said yes it would be prostitution on her part. I had to stay away from that.

Maybe if I offered to pay to be the leading man in her next video? Might work, but did I really want to be in a video where God alone knew who might see me. I could just imagine the uproar if my family were ever to find out. And to be brutally honest, there was no way my modest sexual equipment could match up to the studs Kristal played with in her films. Didn't need to go there. No, I needed to find some other way.

I thought about the problem for a couple of days without coming up with a good idea and then out of the blue, a comment by a co-worker gave me a thought. Jack Duncan has a social function to go to and he needed a date. The problem was that Jack was gay and didn't know any girls. We all knew of Jack's proclivities, but none of the people at the function he was going to knew about his sexual preferences and he didn't want them to know. Sally Ingram told him that all he had to do was call an escort service and hire an escort for the night. Tip the girl well and she would hang all over him, say whatever he asked her to say and make it look like she was the love of his life. Jack went right to the phone book, made a call and then took the rest of the afternoon off to go down to the escort agency.

Why wouldn't that work for me? I wondered how much it would take to get Kristal to be my escort for a week or two if I could even get her to consider it. It might work if I played it right, but to make sure I played it right I would need information – lots of information. I decided on a plan of action and then I stopped and stepped back to re-evaluate. It would be costly. I knew that it would not be cheap so the question became did I really want my fantasy bad enough to spend whatever it took to make it happen? Then I asked myself how often was someone able to make their fantasy come true. In the end the decision was simple.

"Fuck it. Its only money."

And, my fantasy would be paid for courtesy of Joan and Jake.

~–***~–

The first order of business was to hire a detective agency. I asked my attorney for a recommendation and then called and made an appointment. The information I needed wasn't necessarily hidden, but I'm sure that some of it was not exactly public, but I knew that even if I could find it, it would take more of my time than I wanted to spend so I decided to give the job to the professionals.

I met with the man at the agency and told him what I wanted and he said "no problem" and I gave him a retainer and left. Three days later, they called me and gave me what I had asked for.

- Kristal was not married and had no current boyfriend.

- Agent's name and telephone number.

- Kristal was paid on the average of $2500.00 per video.

- Kristal made $156,670.00 last year off of nine videos, adult product endorsements and dancing at topless bars on celebrity's nights.

- And most important to me – she had no history of drug use and from what the detectives had been able to find she had never used drugs.

I already knew from what I'd found on the Net that her real name was Krista Grabowski; that she had been born on September 1, 1972 which made her thirty-seven and that she was five foot six and one hundred and five pounds arranged 34D x 24 x 33.

Armed with the information, I called Kristal's agent, told him I had a business proposition for Kristal and asked him for an appointment. When he asked what kind of a proposition, I told him that all I could tell him over the phone was that it was legal and would pay $8000.00 a week for a minimum of three weeks and could possibly go for as long as six weeks. Even at 10% his commission would be a minimum of $2400.00 so I figured that he would at least give me the appointment so we could talk about it and he did.

I flew to Los Angeles, took a cab to the address that the agent gave me and then I laid it all out for him.

"I want to hire Kristal to be arm candy for me. I know it is an unusual request, but I am willing to pay handsomely for it. It would be for a minimum of three weeks, but it could go as long as six weeks depending on whether or not she has other contractual obligations. I'm offering $8000.00 a week plus all expenses. It is a good deal for her. I know she makes about $2500.00 a film and makes about two a month so what I am offering is more than she would make for the month. I need to make one thing perfectly clear here. There is no sex involved in this. All she has to do is be seen with me, be seen staying with me – in the spare bedroom of course – and to act as if she is crazy about me. Shouldn't be too hard. She is an actress right?"

"I'm not sure that she will even go along with the idea, but before I even approach her on the idea we need to talk money. It might be true that she only makes a couple of films a month and your figure of $2500.00 is low by the way, but she has other income from personal appearances and other activities."

I had come to the meeting knowing that I was going to have to dicker and my $8000.00 offer was just to open the ball. I came into the meeting prepared to go as high as $15000.00 a week and after a half hour of haggling we settled on $12000.00 a week. All that was left was to put the proposal to Kristal and see if she would go for it. I told him that I would be at the Beverly Wilshire and would await his call.

The call came at six that evening. "She is not opposed to the idea, but she wants to meet with you. She has reserved a table at Spago's for eight. Try not to be late. She is a stickler when it comes to punctuality."

I took a cab to the restaurant getting there twenty minutes early and then I walked around sightseeing until five minutes before eight. I was led right to her table and she rose to greet me and offered me her hand. I surprised her and kissed it in the Continental manner and then we sat down. I looked across the table at her and could not believe that I was that close to her. Hell, I couldn't even believe that I'd touched her hand.

There were a good half dozen Hollywood beauties in the place that you have seen in the movies and on TV shows, but in my eyes Kristal's beauty put them all to shame and I wasn't the only man in the room who thought so. I saw male eyes constantly looking our way and I was pretty sure that they were not looking at me. Kristal was obviously amused at my discomfort and so she took pity on me and opened the conversation.

"I'll tell you upfront that I probably won't do what you want, but I was intrigued enough by the proposition that I just had to sit down and talk with you. Jerry tells me that you want me to be what amounts to your escort for three or more weeks and you are willing to pay me $12000.00 a week to do it. Do I have that right?"

I nodded a yes and she said "Why on Earth would you do that when you could get a girl from an escort agency for a third of that amount?"

I figured that I had one shot at it and I figured that the best way to go about it would be to tell the entire story. Who knows, maybe she would be sympathetic and do what I hoped she would do out of pity. I told her about Annalise and Joan and that soured on women I'd retreated to my computer. I told her the effect that she had on me when I found her on the Net and about the fantasies that followed.

"And fantasies is all that they would ever have been had it not been for the money I received from suing Joan's lover and their employer. Then I got to thinking about the fact that you got paid to perform and the men in your films were paid to perform so why not use that windfall money to see if I could live out my fantasy."

"That's the part I don't understand. Jerry said that you said there would be no sex involved. You are willing to pay $12000.00 a week to live out a fantasy; a fantasy that you say revolves around sex with me, but you say no sex. That just does not compute."

"I know, but the more I thought about it the more I realized that if you agreed to do it, to spend the three weeks with me, having sex would cheapen the experience. To be blunt, that would make it no better than hiring a prostitute for an evening. I want more than that. I want the memory of having spent three weeks with the most beautiful woman in the world. I want the memory of walking into the auditorium to attend the symphony with you on my arm and dancing the night away with you at The Pit. I want to remember you sitting next to me at the ballgame and sitting across from me as we have dinner at Antoine's. I want the pleasure of seeing you walk out of the water at Lake Andrews with the sun behind you as you walk toward me. I could go on, but I think you get the idea."

"And it wouldn't hurt you at all to have all your friends and your ex-wife see it happen, would it?"

"I honestly had not thought of that, but yes, it would be an added benefit."

"If I were to agree to your proposal, what would be the mechanics of it?"

"In addition to the weekly sum, I would pay all of your expenses and that includes any shopping that you might do while you are with me. I have a three-bedroom condo and you will have your choice of rooms to sleep in. I only have two weeks of vacation coming so one of the weeks you would be there, I would have to work so I will furnish you with a car to use while I'm at work so you can go shopping or sightseeing or whatever. Those are just some of the things I've thought of. I'm sure that you might think of some others and all you need to do is tell me and I'll do my best to make it happen."

"Mind you I'm not saying yes, but when do you want this to happen?"

"It depends entirely on you and your schedule."

"Jerry said it might go more than three weeks?"

"I told him three and maybe as long as six."

"Why the maybe?"

"I said three to six before we talked money. I didn't know if I would be able to swing more than three until I knew what it would cost."

"And now?"

"I can go six, but that would depend not on me but you. I have no idea of whether you would be able to stay that long. Even if you were to agree to do it, you may not even want to stay the three. My position has to be one of 'I'll take what I can get.'"

"Again, I'm not saying yes, but I'm not saying no either. I'll have to sit down and talk things over with Jerry. I need to see what other commitments I have coming up."

I didn't see how she did it, but she made some sign or other and the waiter magically appeared. "The veal scaloppini here is excellent," she said and I understood that the business part of the meeting was over.

I flew back home knowing that I had come as close to my fantasy as I was ever going to get. I'd met my Goddess; I'd kissed her hand and enjoyed her company for dinner. When you got right down to it I'd gotten more out of the deal than I'd any right to expect. It was time to get on with my life.

~~***~~

A week after I'd returned from LA, I received a phone call from Kristal. Not her agent, but Kristal herself.

"I've decided to do it, but not the way you want. I've checked out my calendar and I do have some open time, but I don't have any three-week blocks that don't have something that I simply have to do. If you are willing to break the weeks up – a week here, a week there – we can work something out. Does that sound like something you might be interested in?"

Talk about your silly questions. "Hell yes," I said. "When?"

"Jerry will call you and work out the details. Now look, this is important. Jerry doesn't know I'm calling you and you can't let him know that I have. He will tell you what I just told you, but then he is going to tell you that in order for it to happen you need to sign an employment contract and a waiver. The waiver will be written in a bunch of legal gobbledygook that you won't understand and Jerry will explain it away as an industry standard that prevents authorities from coming after us for prostitution. What it actually will be is a document waiving all of your rights to the story idea."

"The story idea?"

"Yes. Jerry was joking with a producer about your visit and the producer thought it would be great idea for a film."

"A film?"

"You bet. The producer thinks it will make a great movie and make some big bucks, but you won't get a dime of it if you sign that waiver. The employment contract is the same deal. Jerry will say that it is what prevents us from being charged with prostitution and that is true enough, but part of the employment contract states that all ideas and other things developed while under contract becomes the property of the company."

"But if I don't sign, won't Jerry stop my fantasy from happening?"

"No sweetie. The producer wants the idea and is after Jerry to get it for him. Jerry will want to get it for free, but he will deal if he has to. Jerry also represents some mainstream actors and he will want to stay on the good side of the producer."

"I don't understand. It is an idea or at least a thought that thousands of people have had."

"Yes sweetie, but you brought it out into the open. You talked to an agent about it. You talked to me about it and who knows who else you might have discussed it with. You made it a legitimate idea and if they made the movie without you signing off on it you could sue. A suit like that in this town could run into the hundreds of thousands of dollars and the producer does not want to chance that kind of money or the possible adverse publicity. I know it sounds weird but people are always suing someone over the use of 'their' idea and a good portion of them either win or settle for decent money out of court."

"Why are you telling me this? Aren't you cutting your own throat?"

"No sweetie. I'm only being used as a tool in this. I'm being used as a way to get you to sign the waiver."

"But if there is big money to be made in the film aren't you costing yourself a bunch of change?"

"What it is sweetie is that the producer makes mainstream films and no way is a porn actress going to get anywhere near the project. I may make a few bucks as an un-credited technical advisor, but someone like Catherine Zeta-Jones will be the star and the male lead will be someone like Brad Pitt. It will be a romantic comedy about some country bumpkin who hits the lottery and then comes to Hollywood to make his fantasy come true."

"How would you be a technical advisor?"

"What will happen is that Jerry will have me keep a diary of everything that you and I do and that diary will form the story line. In the end, the boy and girl will discover that they are in love and live happily ever after. But for it to work you have to sign the waiver or be on board with the project."

"Be on board? What does that mean?"

"It means you negotiate a deal."

"What kind of deal?"

"That is up to you sweetie. Just know that if you play your cards right your fantasy is a sure thing. Got to run sweetie. Take care and remember that you haven't talked with me."

~~***~~

Make a deal? What did I know about making deals with a Hollywood agent? I was going to have to fake it, but to fake it I would need to know more than I did. My brother John worked for an advertising agency and he occasionally had to work with some film people so I gave him a call and asked him to meet me for lunch. I could talk to John about damned near anything. When I was eighteen and he was nineteen, we double dated with the Anson twins and he did Bev on the backseat while I was busy doing Barb on the front. The following weekend it was me in the back with Bev and John getting down with Barb. My first threesome was with John and Carrie who was his girlfriend at the time. There weren't many I could talk with about my fantasy, but of those I could John was at the top of the list.

I met him at Mario's and over lunch I explained my problem and he, bless him, had the solution.

"I'll talk to Andy Nelson this afternoon. He is the guy who handles coordinating all of the film work that we do. I'll get the name of an agent from him. When this guy Jerry calls, tell him that you talked about your fantasy with me. Tell him who I work for and that you told me your fantasy and that I said it sounded like it would make a good movie. Tell him I put you in touch with Andy who gave you the name of an agent to call. Tell Jerry that you haven't had a chance to call the agent yet and then like your lady said, it will be up to you to make a deal. Word of advice bro. Take his first offer, triple it and go from there."

"But I don't really want anything but the time with Kristal."

"He doesn't know that. Deal to get more weeks with the babe. Cut what you have to pay and have more to spend on her. Maybe get him to pick up expenses like airfare. Don't know brother mine; you need to figure it out. You know what you want so do what you think you need to do to get it."

He called me that night with the name of an agent in Los Angeles and then I waited to hear from Jerry.

~~***~~

It was two days after Kristal's call that Jerry called me. The conversation went just as Kristal had predicted and when Jerry got to the part about signing waivers and employment contracts I told him that I would have to hold off on that.

"You know we won't be able to move forward on your proposed arrangement with Kristal until we have these papers signed."

"I know, but I found out that I might have some other options available."

"Other options?"

I told him about talking to my brother, my brother bringing Andy into it and Andy giving me the name of an agent in Los Angeles.

"So you are saying that this guy who works with your brother sees a movie in this?"

"Well, he does work with film crews when making commercials and he is exposed to a lot of Hollywood types. He thinks it might have possibilities and he suggested that I give an agent a call. He gave me the name of a guy he has dealt with. Myron Eubanks; know him?"

"We've met. You know, he might be onto something. The more I think about it the more I can see that maybe there is something there. But hey, why call another agent; you already know me. I'll fax you the forms to fill out making me your agent. I'll shop the idea around and see what we can come up with. You need to know that as your agent I get 15% off the top."

"Okay, fax me the paperwork and I'll sign it and get it back to you. Now what about the deal with Kristal?"

"I talked with her a couple of days back and I think we are a go."

Then he went on to explain that I wouldn't get my three weeks in a single block, but if I was willing to split them up I could get the six that we had talked originally talked about.

"We just need to work out the details. Her first open week is the week after next."

Two days later, Jerry called me and told me to submit my idea to him as a proposal. "Your brother's friend has good instincts. There is some interest. Make it look like a screenplay if you can."

What the hell did I know about screenplays? I had however done enough outlines when I was in school to know how to outline an idea. I took what Kristal had told me and changed it around enough so it wouldn't sound like I was repeating something that I'd heard.

My hero was hung up on Kate Hudson and collected her photos, saw all of her movies, read everything written about her in People, US Weekly, Star' In Touch and other magazines like that and in general was obsessed with her (much the same as I was with Kristal). He had a rich uncle who died and left him a ton of money so he decided to head off to Hollywood to see if he could use his newfound wealth to get close to his fantasy woman. He located his fantasy woman's agent and offered him fifty thousand if he would arrange for our hero to work with her in one of her films. The agent took the money, called in a favor and got our hero a bit part in one of fantasy woman's films. Then the agent laughingly told a bunch of people about 'the idiot' who paid just to be near fantasy woman and fantasy woman overheard, felt sorry for our hero and made an effort to spend some time with him on the set.

She invited him to a party at her house and he went and had a good time. He asked her for a date and she said yes and they had a good time. Romance bloomed. Then the busy bodies got involved. "You are ruining your career." "Your public will never stand for you getting together with a loser like him." People started doing things to 'save her from herself.' Things like deliberately scheduling her for things when they knew she had a date with him. Things like leaking phony stories to the gossip press about her 'secret romance' with_____(fill in the blank with the name of the male Hollywood star of the moment). Things like leaking to gossip columnists that she only spends time with our hero to camouflage her romance with the male star of the moment.

Our hero hears all of this and his heart is broken and he leaves the Left Coast and goes home to Hicksville to lick his wounds. A couple of weeks later, there is a knock on his door and he opens it to find fantasy woman standing there. She rushes into his arms and they live happily ever after. Or not. I faxed the outline off to Jerry and then waited to see what would happen next.

~~***~~

What happened next caught me completely by surprise. It was a week after I'd faxed my outline to Jerry. It was a Saturday night when the phone rang and it was Kristal.

"My flight leaves here at 3:06 pm tomorrow and gets into Denver at 6:21. You going to pick me up or should I cab over to your place? If I have to cab I'll need your address."

I was stunned into speechlessness.

"Rob? Are you there?"

I finally managed to get my wits about me and said, "I'll be there to pick you up. You won't be able to miss me. I'll be the one with the big goofy grin who won't be able to stand still."

It didn't really hit me until after I'd hung up the phone. My silly fantasy, my ridiculous pipe dream, my stupid off the wall idea was going to happen. It was really going to happen.

I was at the airport when United Flight 748 arrived, but because of all the dumb Homeland Security bullshit I couldn't meet Kristal at the gate, but I told her that I would be outside waiting. She came out the door and all eyes were on her as she looked right and then left and spotted me. She walked up to me, put her two suitcases down, put her arms around me and gave me a kiss that made me weak in the knees.

"Happy to see me?"

"Oh God, yes."

"Well then lover, let's get out of here and start our week."

Chapter 2

On the way to my condo Kristal said, "I don't know how you did it, but you really put Jerry's panties in a twist. He's all upset over you not going along with the program."

"I owe it all to you. Your phone call is what got me going."

I explained to her my getting with John and the outcome of our talk.

"What I don't understand is what caused you to get on the phone and clue me in?"

"Simple sweetie. You seemed like a nice guy and Jerry was getting ready to do to you what Hollywood always does to nice guys. Screw them. They have stuck it to me a time or two and I saw it as my chance to get a little payback. That and you are kind of cute."

"Me? Cute?"

"Don't sell yourself short sweetie. If it was just the money I would have taken a pass on this deal. You might not think so, but you do have something going for you. So, tell me what we will be doing this week."

I laid it all out for her and she told me that what she had packed would work for most of it, but if I was doing a tux and a limo for the symphony, she was going to have to come up with an evening gown.

"I guess that will be the first order of business in the morning."

When we got to my condo, I carried her bags in and showed her to her room. I showed her where everything was and while she was in the bathroom freshening up from her trip I got the pitcher of martinis out of the fridge and poured two glasses. I had checked with Jerry and found out some of her likes and dislikes and her favorite drink was a martini with the little onion. I had it ready for her when she came into the room.

She took it, sat down on the couch next to me, tucked her legs up under her and asked, "What's the plan for tomorrow?"

"Get up when we get up. I'll fix breakfast and then we will go shopping for your evening gown. Have lunch and then I'll expose you to some of my friends and hope that you won't come away thinking too badly about me."

"That should be interesting. Just what are they going to do that might cause me to think poorly of you?"

"Just be themselves. They can be a pretty crude bunch when they have had a beer or three."

"So if you are afraid of what they might do why are you going to take me to meet them?"

"It is one of those rock and hard place things. Before I had a clue that my fantasy would come true or that it would happen this week, I organized a 'guy's afternoon out'. I arranged a skybox for tomorrow's Rockies game. It is my outing so I have to go, but now that you are here there isn't any way I'm not going to make the most of every minute I can spend with you."

"Well sweetie, for your information, I can do crude so don't worry about me."

She finished her martini and said, "I'm beat sweetie. It has been a long day for me and I'm going to turn in."

She stood up, leaned down and kissed me on the cheek and then went to her room. I went to bed thinking that I might never wash that cheek ever again.

~~***~~

The morning was a revelation. I had never seen Kristal without her makeup and her hair done just right. All of her photos were glamour shots and in all of her films she was made up to look her best. The night we had dinner and when I met her at the airport she was perfection personified.

When she wandered into the kitchen in an oversized Michigan State sweatshirt, flip flops, no makeup and 'bed' hair, she looked totally different. Put a picture of her the way she looked that morning next to one of her glamour shots and you would never know that they were the same person. Even though just out of bed and not at her best, she was still breathtaking beautiful. I fed her scrambled eggs with cheese, bacon, fried potatoes and sourdough toast and after three cups of coffee, she got up to shower and dress.

She poured through the sports pages of the Rocky Mountain News while I drove us to Park Meadows Mall and then we spent the better part of the morning and early afternoon hitting shops. She eventually found the dress she wanted and on our way out to the car we passed a sports shop and told me to wait and she would be right back. She went into the store and came out ten minutes later with a package. I gave her a questioning look and she smiled at me and said, "Later."

We hit a Red Robin for lunch and talked some more about what we would be doing that week. She was especially nervous about having dinner at my brother's on Wednesday because my parents and older sister would be there.

"What is your family going to think about you being with me?"

"Don't forget that it was John's plan that took care of Jerry. He knows about you and he thinks it is fantastic. As for mom, dad and my sister what are the odds that they watch porn films? Even if they do would I have proposed doing what we are doing if I cared about what other people would think? Besides, my parents are too well mannered to make you feel uncomfortable even if they do know who you are."

"What about your sister?"

"She has always considered her little brother a dork. If she knows who you are and sees us together it will knock her back on her heels."

"I'm not worried about me sweetie. I've had a long time to get used to how some people look at me. I know you don't care about your buddies, but family is different."

"Thank you for worrying about it, but I know my family and I'm not concerned."

We went home, changed clothes and headed for Coors Field. Kristal was wearing jeans, tennis shoes and a windbreaker even though it was fairly warm outside and I asked her why she had it on. She smiled at me and told me that she had heard that Denver turned chilly in the evenings at times and she wanted to be prepared.

When we walked into the box, the guys who were already there turned to the door and you could see the jaws drop when I walked in with Kristal. "Guys, this is Kristal," and then I introduced her to the guys and said:

"I know this is supposed to be a guy's outing, but Kristal flew in from Los Angeles to spend a few days with me and I couldn't just leave her alone at the condo."

I could tell from the looks on the faces of Charlie and Troy that they knew who Kristal was and I wondered how the afternoon was going to play out. It didn't take long for things to get interesting. The Rockies were playing the Giants that day and as the Giants took the field, Kristal put her fingers in her mouth and gave a loud whistle. The she hollered, "Kick ass guys! Kick some Rocky Mountain ass!" as she shed her windbreaker and displayed the Giant's jersey that she had apparently bought at Park Meadows. She looked around the room, gave a 1000 watt smile and said:

"What can I say guys. I'm a California girl."

The tight jeans and jersey did nothing to hide or disguise her 34D-23-34 body from the guys and I'm sure that baseball was the farthest thing from their minds at that moment. I saw Charlie and Troy looking at me with dumbfounded looks on their faces as I moved up to Kristal and put my arms around her and hugged her.

"You should have warned me about this."

"What?" she laughed, "And spoil the surprise?"

She pulled my head down and kissed me on the lips, winked at me and then we settled in to watch the game.

There was a lot of good-natured ribbing between Kristal and the guys and Kristal gave better than what she got. All in all it was a fun afternoon made better by the Rockies winning. The guys ragged on Kristal about the Left Coast Losers and then Kristal surprised the hell out of everyone there, including me, when she went up to Jonas who was the only one there wearing a Rockies jersey and took her Giants jersey off.

She handed it to Jonas and as everyone stared at her tits barely contained by her bra she said, "Here. Trade you."

Jonas stared at her cleavage for several seconds before grabbing her jersey and taking his off and handing it to her. He held it to his nose, sniffed it. "I'll never wash it and I'll sleep with it under my pillow for the rest of my life."

Kristal kissed him on the cheek and then she slipped on the Rockies jersey. Jonas was 6 foot four and his jersey fell below her knees and she laughed. "I have a new nightgown."

She picked up her windbreaker and said "Thanks guys! I had a good time." Then she turned to me and said, "Take me home Rob. I'm horny."

We walked out leaving nine guys looking at each other and shaking their heads in disbelief. As we walked to the car Kristal said:

"How did I do sweetie?"

"You were magnificent."

"Yeah, I was, wasn't I?"

~~***~~

We had dinner at a Denny's and then we went back to my condo. I poured her a martini and we curled up on the couch and watched TV until she yawned and said she was going to turn in. I watched the idiot box for another half hour and then I went to bed. I spent some time staring up at the ceiling reliving the day and wondering how it might change my life. I knew one thing for sure. There were nine guys who were never going to look at me the same way again.

The next morning, I woke to the sounds of noise coming from the kitchen. I got up to find Kristal rummaging in the cupboards. All she had on was the Rockies jersey and she still looked fantastic, sleepy hair and all. She heard me come into the room and without turning she asked, "Where do you keep the Bisquick? I'm going to make pancakes."

I showed her where it was and then I went and took my morning shower. Kristal stuck her head in the room as I was toweling myself dry and asked me how many hotcakes I would like and I saw her looking at my exposed penis as I told her three or four and since I had never seen her in any of her videos with anything less than huge I wondered if she was thinking, *"Poor guy. Only six inches. No wonder his wife wanted to try a bigger one."*

Thankfully I had long ago realized that there was nothing you could do about what you were born with and having a big dick just meant that you were born lucky. I thought of the joke about the hooker who laughed at the small cock on her customer and asked him who he expected to satisfy "with that tiny thing." The customer looked her right in the eye and said "Me." That was my attitude. I would always do my best to get my partner off and if that meant burying my head up to the neck in her pussy and licking it from the inside I'd go for it, but when it came to getting me off what I had did the job just fine. Besides, if Kristal felt sorry for me for only having six and five-eight inches, it didn't matter since I'd already made it clear that sex was not part of the deal.

Then I looked in the mirror and thought, "Get a grip Rob. For all you know she might have walked away pissed because you didn't get an instant hard on as soon as you saw her walk in." I finished in the bathroom and walked into the kitchen and she set a plate with four hotcakes down in front of me and then sat down across from me. As she nibbled on her lone pancake she asked:

"What's on for today?"

"The limo will pick us up at six-fifteen. Until then the day is yours. What would you like to do?"

"My cousin used to drive in the race to the top of Pike's Peak, but I have never been there. Is it close enough that we could go there and be back in time?"

"We can be there in an hour and a half. If we leave in the next half hour we can make it."

It was a very enjoyable day. I'm lucky that I didn't kill us on the drive because I kept taking my eyes off the road and looking over at Kristal sitting next to me. I know it was silly of me. I mean she was there and I knew she was there, but I had to keep looking to confirm that it wasn't a daydream – a figment of my imagination.

We spent an hour on the top of the Peak and she bought a couple of souvenir t-shirts at the gift shop. While we were there I led her over to one of the telescopes that were mounted on pedestals and pointed it southwest.

"If you look real hard you can see the roof of the little cabin I have over by Evergreen Station."

"A cabin? Can we go there?"

"Not this time, we need to get back in time for the symphony, but I'll take you there on one of the next weeks you are here. I'll warn you ahead of time that you will be roughing it. There is no electricity, no running water and an outhouse for a bathroom."

"I can rough it. I want to go. Can't we go now? Do we really have to go to the symphony?"

"No honey, we don't have to go to the symphony, but I didn't pack for the cabin. I don't have any of the things we will need if we are going there. I promise you that we will go there the next time you are here."

"I'm going to hold you to that. I like the mountains."

~~***~~

The limo driver knocked on the door at exactly six-fifteen and I called out to Kristal that it was time to go. My jaw dropped when she came out of her room. She was stunning. It was a good thing that the symphony was a listening event because if it was a visual event no one would see any of it. All eyes and I do mean all eyes – male and female – were going to be on my date.

It started as soon as we stepped out the door. The driver of the limo could not take his eyes off of Kristal. He stumbled a couple of times on his way to open the rear door for us because he wasn't watching where he was walking and instead kept glancing at Kristal. I wasn't sure that I wanted him to drive because I knew he would have his eyes on the rear view mirror instead of the road. By the time we reached the car, I knew for sure that I didn't want him to drive and I got a big grin on my face.

It was silly of me, but the whole thing was silly. My idea and Kristal's acceptance of it were off the wall to begin with so why not a little more weirdness. When we reached the limo, he opened the door for Kristal and then I told him to get in back with her. He protested until I slipped him a fifty and then he got in back and took the seat opposite Kristal while she looked at me with a bemused smile. I got in, started the limo and drove away.

When we got to the auditorium, the people on the sidewalk saw a man in a tux get out of the limo, walk to the rear door and open it. A stunningly beautiful woman got out followed by a man in a chauffer's uniform. The man in the tux offered the beautiful lady his arm and then they walked into the building. At least sixty people saw it happen and I'm sure that most of them are still trying to get their minds around it.

As we took our seats Kristal asked me, "Why in the world did you do that?"

"He couldn't take his eyes off you. He would have been looking in the rear view all the way here and God only knows who he might have hit. Besides, just imagine how it will play in the movie after Jerry and his producer buddy read about it in your diary."

The evening's performance was a dual program of Beethoven's First and Fifth symphonies. I was totally knocked on my ass when just before the start of the Fifth, Kristal leaned to me and said:

"You should pay particular attention when the opening measure introduces the piccolo, contrabassoon and three trombones at the same time. That is quite a departure from Beethoven's usual style."

I don't know jack about classical music other than I know I like to listen to it so I sat there and looked at her, open mouthed. She smiled at me and said:

"What? You think all I am is a hot body and a pretty face?"

There was a cocktail party at the Brown Palace after the performance and Kristal shone. The men and women in attendance could not take their eyes off of her. The men looked at her with lust in their hearts and the women looked at her with hatred in their eyes and all of them, men and women alike, wondered what a woman like that was doing on the arm of a guy like me.

I was waiting at the bar waiting on the bartender to build us two fresh drinks while I watched Kristal in conversation with Riccardo Muti who was the visiting conductor who had conducted the evening's performance when Bill Thomas walked up to me.

"I never knew that you had that large of a dick."

"Why would you say that?"

"Why else would Kristal Summers be with you?"

"She likes my smile."

"Yeah, right. You have to let me in on your secret."

Before I could say anything, Kristal walked up to us and I handed her her fresh martini. I introduced her to Bill and then Bill said:

"I just have to ask this. What is a drop dead gorgeous woman doing with a guy like Rob? I mean he is a really great guy and all, but…" and before he could finish what he was going to say Kristal interrupted him and said:

"He is great in bed."

Bill's jaw dropped and Kristal took me by the arm and said, "Come on lover, there is someone I want you to meet," and she led me over to Muti. As we walked away from Bill she said:

"I think your stock just went up a few points. Hope you don't mind."

"Not in the least. Just having him hear you call me lover made my evening perfect."

After we settled into the limo I said, "There is something I have always wanted to do. Will you give me your panties?"

"Are you that kinky? You want to sniff my panties?"

"No, nothing like that."

She lifted her dress and took off her panties and I saw her pussy live for the first time. Before then I had only seen it on my downloaded videos. I had to tear my eyes away from it when she handed me her panties. I rapped on the partition and when the driver lowered it I handed him the undergarment and told him to put them over the rear view mirror.

He did what I told him to do and as the partition slid back up Kristal asked, "What did you do that for?"

"For the same reason I drove earlier. I want to arrive alive at our destination and he just can't take his eyes off of you. For that matter I can't either, but I need for his eyes to be on the road."

"You know what he will think is going on back here don't you?"

"It will give him something to tell his buddies."

When we got back to the condo, I tipped the driver handsomely and then we went inside and changed out of our evening clothes. I put on sweats and Kristal joined me on the couch wearing her Rockies jersey. We sipped martinis and she filled me in on Hollywood gossip and I filled her in on my career as a civil engineer. She wanted to talk about Joan, but I shut that down in a hurry.

"It is still a very raw open wound and I don't need to go there."

She told me that she knew how it felt because she had gone through something similar.

"I didn't get to see it like you did, but someone who did see it told me and when I confronted him he didn't even try to deny it. He just shrugged his shoulders and acted like it was no big thing."

That made no sense to me. Why would anyone who had a woman like Kristal be playing around with someone else? We talked a little more and then called it a night.

~~***~~

Wednesday, I took Kristal out for breakfast and then we spent a good part of the day lying around the condo complex's swimming pool. Spending a good part of the day looking at Kristal in a bikini was almost enough in itself to make the week worthwhile. Because of the major, major wood that it caused, I spent a good part of that time lying on my stomach and don't think for one second that Kristal didn't know why.

We arrived at John's house at five and found that my sister and her husband were already there. John swore to me that he didn't tell his wife Nancy anything at all about Kristal other than I would be bringing a date to the family dinner and when Nancy and Kristal were introduced I saw no sign that Nancy has a clue as to Kristal was. It was a different story with my sister Rachel and her husband. There was no doubt from the look on Kevin's face that he knew who Kristal was. I couldn't read the look on Rachel's face. It could have been that she knew who Kristal was or it just could have been shock and surprise that her dork of a brother could even know a woman like Kristal. I know Kristal read the faces the same as I did, but I had no way of knowing what she was thinking.

We sipped martinis and talked for a while and then Nancy got up to see about dinner and Kristal got up and said she would give Nancy a hand. Rachel looked from me to Kristal and then back to me again and then she got up to join Nancy and Kristal in the kitchen. Kevin was just bursting to say something, but he couldn't because John was there and he didn't know that John already knew about Kristal. John could read people and he knew what was roaring around in Kevin's head, but he wasn't going to say anything.

He just smiled and said, "When you told me about her and described her, I thought you were probably on drugs, but now that I've seen her I can honestly say that your description did not do her justice. Where in the world did you meet her?"

I gave him the cover story that Kristal and I had agreed on. "I was in Los Angeles on business a month or so ago and I met her while I was out there."

Before I could say anymore, mom and dad came into the room. Mom looked around and then said, "Okay, where is she? Where is this girl who is so special that we are having a family dinner in the middle of the week just so we can meet her?"

John laughed and said, "Get real mom. We set this dinner up before we even knew about Rob's new lady friend. Anyway, the girls are in the kitchen."

Mom headed off for the kitchen and dad sat down and as was usual with him the talk immediately turned to sports and stayed on that subject until mom came back into the room with Kristal and introduced her to dad. I saw his eyebrows rise as he looked at her and then at me. I read the look.

"You're shitting me! You and my boy? No way! Just what the hell is going on here?"

But dad was too well mannered to say what he was thinking and so he just shook Kristal's hand and said, "Nice meeting you."

At that point, Nancy called us all to dinner. Naturally, mom being mom, the table conversation started off with mom asking:

"And just how did you two meet?"

We knew it was coming and we were ready for it. Kristal said "I was walking down the street in Beverly Hills when one of my heels got caught in a crack in the sidewalk. I stumbled, twisted my ankle, started to fall and luckily Rob was there to catch me. He helped me to a seat at a table at one of the outdoor cafes and one thing led to another and we had dinner that night. When I knew I was coming to Denver, I gave Rob a call and he offered to show me around while I'm here."

"What have you seen?" Nancy asked and as soon as Kristal said that I had taken her to a Rockies game my dad jumped in and it was sports talk again and Kristal wound dad up when she told him that the Rockies were a second rate team compared to the Giants and the conversation that followed was lively indeed until dinner was over and it was time to clear the table. Kristal got up to help Nancy as did mom and Rachel and the men moved to the living room.

The funniest part of the evening for me was watching Kevin. He was just dying to say something to me, but didn't dare in front of John or my dad. The women finished in the kitchen and joined us in the living room.

After everyone was seated Nancy said, "The reason for this little gathering tonight is that John and I have an announcement to make and we wanted everyone to hear it at the same time. There is going to be a new member in the family."

Everyone turned to look at Kristal and me and my mom gasped. Nancy laughed and said, 'I'm not talking about Rob and Kristal. I'm talking about what will be joining us in a little over eight months.'"

There were congratulations and the talk was off sports for the rest of the evening. After a bit, I said that Kristal and I had to be going and as everyone was saying goodbye to Kristal, my dad looked me in the eye and said, "I sure as hell hope you know what you are doing."

Mom and Kristal walked up to us before I could ask him what he meant. Was it his way of telling me that he knew who Kristal was or was it a "She's out of your league son; make sure you don't get burnt" kind of thing?

As we got in the car Kristal said, "I think that went well. You have a very nice family."

"They seemed to like you."

"Your mother and Nancy invited me to go shopping with them tomorrow."

"What did you tell them?"

"I said that I wasn't sure what your plans were and that I would call them and let them know."

"I had planned on going back up into the mountains and spending the night at the cabin, but I would never come between a woman and her chance to go shopping."

"And this woman would never choose shopping over going to the mountains so I guess that settles that."

When we got home there was a message from Kevin on the answering machine.

"Call me Rob. It is important."

I called him and put the phone on speaker.

"Hello?

"It's Rob Kevin, I got your message. Whatcha need?"

"Jesus Rob, do you have any idea who you brought to dinner tonight?"

"Of course, I do."

"You mean you know that she is a porn star?"

"Who? Kristal? Where did you get an off the wall idea like that?"

"Not shitting you Rob. Her name is Kristal Summers and she is in porn videos."

"Now I know you don't know what you are talking about. Her name is Kristal Grabowski, not Summers."

"Trust me on this one Rob. I've got two of her videos. No mistake Rob; she is Kristal Summers."

"Oh wow. How lucky can you get?"

"What do you mean?"

"Have you got a porn star sleeping at your house?"

"No."

"I guess I have and how lucky is that. Talk to you later, Kevin. Bye."

I smiled at Kristal and said, "Wait until I tell him we are getting married." I saw her face change and quickly said, "I'll just be pulling his leg honey; just jerking his chain."

"How long before all of your family knows?"

I told her what my father said as we were leaving and then told her that by then all of the men probably knew.

"And you don't care?"

"Have you looked at yourself in the mirror lately? What man wouldn't give an arm or a leg to have you on his arm? All it means is that some people will be looking at me now and wondering just what it is that I have that makes me desirable to a porn star. Tell you what. From now on, I want you to answer the phone when it rings. When they ask for me say something like 'Let me see if he has his clothes back on yet.' It will drive them all crazy trying to figure it out."

"You really don't care."

"Not a bit."

"What should I tell them if they ask me point blank?"

"You tell them anything that your little heart desires."

"You are sure about this?"

"Absolutely. But for right now you need to pack for a day and a night in the mountains. Sweatshirt, jeans, tennis shoes, sweater and your windbreaker. It can get pretty chilly up there this time of the year."

~~***~~

The aspen leaves were changing color so the drive to the cabin was colorful. On the dirt road on the way up the mountain we saw several deer and a couple of elk. Kristal spotted a hawk and just after she saw it, it dived and that signaled that some poor rabbit or other small creature had become dinner.

Kristal was surprised when we pulled up at the cabin and she looked around. She must have been thinking of something like the lodges at Lake Tahoe so a small stone cabin with a small wooden deck caught her by surprise.

"I'll admit that it isn't much to look at, but as a weekend get-a-way it works just fine."

I unlocked the door and she went in while I unloaded the water, ice, food and propane tank for the Coleman stove. While I was doing that, Kristal was looking around and shaking her head as I said:

"No electricity, no running water and the heat comes from that wood burning pot-bellied stove over there in the corner."

She pointed to the stairs at the end of the room and I told her that they went up to what served as the bedroom in the loft. She went up the stairs, looked around and came down.

"There is only one bed up there."

"I know. That is where you will sleep. I'll take the couch down here."

We went out onto the deck and sat down and I pointed out the landmarks. "That cone shaped breast looking mountain straight out in front is Mount Pisgah. Just to the left of it is Cripple Creek. You can't see it from here, but at night you will see the town's lights reflected in the sky. That large lump to the far left is Pike's Peak."

"What do you do when you come up here?"

"Take walks, sit on the deck and read or just sit and look at the scenery."

"That's it?"

"If you like peace and quiet it is enough. Come on, I'll show you around."

We went for a long two-hour walk and when we got back I fixed us some lunch and we took it out on the deck to eat it. She spotted another hawk, but this one just circled looking for prey and not finding any it moved off to the south. We sat there and talked for about a half hour and suddenly I became aware that we were holding hands. I've no idea of when or how it happened, but I was not about to do anything that would break the spell. Maybe another hour went by and I caught movement out of the corner of my eye.

"Sit still and don't move," I told Kristal, "And watch the tree line just to your right."

A doe stepped cautiously out from the trees and moved out into the open and seconds later three more followed her and the four of them slowly meandered across the back of the property.

"I've got a couple of salt blocks down in that little dip about a fifty yards down from the deck and just to the left of those dead aspens."

The lead doe came up to where the salt blocks were, glanced in the direction of the deck and then lowered her head to the salt. The four stayed there about fifteen minutes and then wandered off.

"Can we follow them?"

"We can, but we have to be careful to stop when they stop and not make any sudden moves or loud noises or we will spook them."

We followed the four from fifty yards back for about an hour and a half as they wandered around chewing grass and eating the bark off of aspen trees. We started losing the light and turned and went back to the cabin. I fixed dinner and then we sat out on the deck and looked at the stars. I pointed out the North Star, and the Big and Little Dippers and a couple of bright spots that I thought were satellites because they never appeared to blink.

The shocker came at bedtime. I started making up the couch and Kristal said:

"No couch for you tonight fantasy boy. Tonight you share a bed with me."

It was a good thing that I didn't have my hopes up. All she meant was that we would share the queen size bed. She wore sweats and I wore pajamas. One thing about that potbellied stove. When it burned down and the ashes cooled, it got downright chilly up there on the mountain. I woke up around two in the morning and found Kristal spooned up against me for warmth. It was very, very, very hard for me to behave.

On the ride home Kristal said, "This is not turning out the way I expected."

"And just what did you expect?"

"I expected that each night would be a party somewhere so you could show off to as many people as possible."

"My fantasy was to be with you. Just that, to be with you. Alone or with a bunch of people, just to be with you. I couldn't help the ball game because that was already planned before I knew you were coming. Ditto with the dinner at John's house and with Ken's retirement party tonight. To be absolutely honest here, I never expected even in my wildest dreams that this would ever happen so I've just moved on with my life. However, I do plan on taking you out and showing you off on Saturday. We will be going out to dinner and then dancing. I hope you like Mexican food and country western dancing."

"You are full of surprises sweetie. Symphony on one end, country music on the other and peaceful quiet mountains in the middle."

I shrugged and paid attention to my driving.

~~***~~

Sexy and elegant. That is the only way to describe Kristal as she came into the living room ready to go to Ken's retirement party. A simple little black dress, a lone string of pearls and heels. She took my breath away. One thing was sure and that was no one at work was ever going to see me in the same light again. No more would they think "hard working, nose to the grindstone, stick in the mud Rob."

You could hear the momentary hush as Kristal and I walked into the banquet room at the Hyatt. I had no idea if and of the men – or women for that matter – recognized Kristal, but I didn't care if they did. She was on my arm and all was well with my world. I got Kristal a martini from the bar and then we circulated and I introduced her to my coworkers. I didn't strut and I wasn't all puffed up like a peacock, but I have no doubt that everyone there knew how pleased I was over the attention that Kristal and I received.

Then Barry, president and CEO of the company, called out that it was time to eat. After a prime rib dinner, we had a drink and sat and listened to all the speeches and applauded when Ken received his going away gifts – fly rod, creel and an Atlas to use for planning fishing trips and of course, the proverbial gold watch. After that, it broke up into a cocktail party.

I was surprised when Barry came up to us. I had been with the company six years and in all that time Barry had only spoken to me once. After some small talk Barry said, "I hope you aren't going to let this one get away Rob."

I was even more surprised when Kristal laughed and said, "I've been trying to nail him down, but I can't get him to commit."

Barry gave me an appraising glance and then moved off to talk with others. I turned to Kristal.

"Can't get me to commit? We can be in Vegas in four hours and Elvis can do the honors."

"Don't you wish."

The silly part was yes, I did wish.

~~***~~

Saturday was a sleep in day and I didn't roll out of bed until a little after nine. I was making coffee when Kristal came into the room. Barefoot, tousled hair and nothing on but her Rockies jersey. I thought that I could stand seeing her like that for the rest of my life.

She smiled at me. "In or out?"

"In or out what?"

"Breakfast here or out?"

"Which would you prefer?"

"Out. This is a lazy day and neither of us should do anything except lay around the house or pool."

So that is what we did. We had breakfast at a Village Inn and then took the sun by the pool. I'm sure that Kristal in her bikini was the center of attention, but I've no way of knowing for sure since I couldn't take my eyes off of her long enough to see what other people were doing.

After a light lunch we had to go shopping. All Kristal had packed were tennis shoes, flip flops and high heels, none of which were suitable for country western dancing. She didn't want to go the boot route, but we did find a nice pair of flats with leather soles that would work just fine.

We hit Three Margaritas for dinner and then we went to the Wagon Wheel. The live band there that week was Little Jimmy Hansen and the Barnyard Stompers. There were several people there that I knew and we ended up shoving several tables together and I introduced Kristal to everyone. I had gotten out of the habit of checking faces to see if anyone had a clue as to who my date was because I just didn't care.

Kristal could two-step and waltz, but she didn't know any of the line dances and she didn't know western swing so we had a fun evening as we danced and I tried to teach her what I knew. There was a bit of a dark spot when Sally Fortner nudged me and said:

"Don't look now, but your ex just walked in."

Kristal heard her and asked, "Where?"

Sally pointed and I saw Joan sitting down at a table with two of her girlfriends. One of her girlfriends must have seen me and mentioned it to Joan and she looked our way and then quickly turned back to her friends. Kristal and I got up and went over and joined the line for a Tush

Push and when it was over and the band moved into a waltz, Kristal pulled me out onto the floor.

"When we go by her table, I want you molded to me."

"You are evil."

"I know sweetie; it is part of my charm."

We made a dozen turns around the floor and every time we went by Joan's table, Kristal would be nibbling on my ear or nuzzling into my neck. I've no idea how Joan was taking it because I never looked her way. The waltz ended and we went back to our table and after a couple of minutes I got up to use the john and when I came back to the table, I saw Josh Billings walking away from the table and everyone at the table laughing. Josh and I had never been friends. In fact, we couldn't stand each other. Before I could sit down, Kristal stood up and pulled me out onto the floor for a two-step and as we went by Joan's table for the third time Kristal said, "She can't take her eyes off of you."

"So?"

"Nothing sweetie; it was just a comment."

"It is you she is looking at and she is trying to figure out what a bombshell like you is doing with me."

"It is you she is looking at sweetie. Trust me on this one. I know when someone is looking at me and she isn't."

"No, you trust me on this. She isn't looking at me. She had me and I wasn't enough for her. All she is doing is wondering what a woman like you is doing with a guy like me."

Kristal just shrugged and made no reply. About ten minutes later, Ben Fortner asked Kristal to try a two-step with him and when they got out on the floor, Sally pulled me up off my chair and we moved out on the floor.

"Where on Earth did you find her Rob?"

I told her the same story that Kristal had told my family.

"And she flew here just to spend a week with you?"

I shrugged.

"Not that you aren't worth the trip baby, but she does seem to be a bit more than you…oh never mind. I'm happy for you. I like her. We all like her and we love what she did to Josh."

"What did she do to Josh?"

"When you got up to go to the bathroom he came over and asked her for a dance. She politely said no and said her man – that's what she called you, her man – might not like it and to come back when you were there so you could either approve or not. And then Josh, asshole that he is, told her that she was wasting her time on a loser like you; that you weren't even man enough to hang onto your wife. She looked him right in the eye and told him that it wasn't your fault that your wife wasn't woman enough for you. And then she said, and this is an exact quote, "Do you think that I would fly here from LA to spend a week with a guy who couldn't get the job done? Fuck off asshole!' Everybody started laughing and Josh slunk off licking his wounds."

"Go back to the point where you said "never mind." What were you going to say?"

"Don't take this wrong Rob. You know that I love you like a brother, but I don't think the two of you could make it for the long haul. There is just something about her. I don't know what. Just a feeling, but she isn't wife material."

"Maybe that is a good thing. Maybe I'm not husband material so maybe we would be a good fit."

"Whatever baby; have your fun while you can."

We were there another hour and then Kristal said we needed to be going. "I have a noon flight to catch lover and I still have to pack."

We said our goodbyes and as we left I saw Joan watching us leave and I wondered what she was thinking. Sorry that she had fucked it up for us, or wondering how a little dick like me ended up with a woman like Kristal.

Kristal was quiet on the ride home and when we got there she kissed me on the cheek and went to her room. I undressed and was lying there looking up at the ceiling and going over the week in my mind when the bedroom door opened and Kristal came into the room. With the hallway light behind her I could see that she was naked. She walked over to the bed, pulled the covers off of me and got on the bed.

I started to ask her what she was doing but before I could get a word out, she placed a finger across my lips and said, "I know that this isn't supposed to be part of the deal, but I want to do it. I want your fantasy to be perfect."

She took her finger from my lips, lowered her face and kissed me. It was incredible. We did everything but anal. She sucked my cock and I ate her pussy. We did it in the missionary position and when she had me back up for the second time we went cowgirl. We went sixty-nine and the third time was doggie and the forth was reverse cowgirl. The fifth was going to be anal, but my little guy just could not answer the call to duty. I do have to admit that the sex was not physically any better than the sex I had enjoyed with Joan and Annalise, but emotionally it was mind blowing. I actually got to make love to my fantasy woman and that in itself gave me an unbelievable high. We fell asleep wrapped in each other's arms and I slept like a baby.

~~***~~

The ride to the airport was silent for the first half of the trip and then Kristal said, "Your ex would kill to have you back."

"Where did you get that silly idea?"

"From her."

I glanced over at her.

"I followed her into the bathroom last night. I asked her why she was dumb enough to let you get away. She told me that it wasn't dumb; it was just plain stupid. A phone call sweetie and she's yours."

"She was mine once before and I wasn't enough for her."

"Don't give me that sweetie. You were more than enough for her and you know it. The problem here is your ego, your pride, your sense of self-worth or whatever. She let someone else borrow something that you considered yours alone and it pissed you off. Let me tell you something lover. There isn't a woman in the world who hasn't heard that bigger is better and there isn't a woman who has heard that who hasn't wondered if it is true. Most never get the chance to find out and almost all who do get the chance take it. I know at least a dozen married women who have taken the chance, satisfied their curiosity without their husbands knowing and then have gone back to being loving and faithful wives."

"You know a dozen?"

"You've seen who I work with lover and you've seen what they have. We travel in the same circles so I see who they date and run around with. But here is the thing about huge cocks. The guys they are attached to are pursued by women who want to 'know' and they don't have to work for their pussy the way guys like you have to. They don't have to go the 'wine and dine' route. They don't need to buy the flowers, cards and candy. They don't need to do any romancing so all the girl gets out of the deal is fucked. She finds out that bigger is indeed better, but that all the guy has to offer is a big dick and for most women that just isn't enough. They need love and affection and they need to be treated as a person and not just a piece of willing meat.

"Your ex took the chance and satisfied her curiosity and if you hadn't found out, it would have been over and done with and believe it or not your marriage would have been a lot stronger for it because she would have realized just what she had in you and what you brought to the table. You were the complete package and not just a large piece of meat.

"But you did find out and pride and ego got into it. One more thing lover and then I'll shut up. I saw it and I know that one or two others at our table saw it. Any time you thought no one was looking your way you were looking at your ex. Deny it all you want, but something is still there."

By then we were at the departure area and I pulled over and got Kristal's suitcases out of the trunk. She put her arms around me and gave me one hell of a hot kiss and then she said, "I had a blast lover and I'm glad I did it, but the bad news is that this is all there is going to be. No three or more weeks. One is all I can give and I hope it was memorable. Goodbye lover and good luck."

She kissed me again and then I watched her walk away.

~~***~~

The following weeks were full of phone calls from people asking, "Do you have the slightest idea of who that was?" I couldn't stop for a drink after work without someone saying "You lucky dog you. How in the hell did you meet her?" Some women that I had been interested in at one time or another, but who hadn't been interested in me were saying, "Call me. Maybe we can do lunch."

I spent my nights reliving my week with Kristal and wishing that it could have lasted longer. If it would have it wouldn't have led to anything and I knew it. Kristal hadn't hidden her nature from me. One of the nights we sat on the couch and sipped martinis she told me why she was in 'the business.'

"I love sex, I love variety, I love size and I get it all and get paid for it. For me it just doesn't get any better than that."

Still, I could fantasize about a life with her and I did.

Three days after Kristal flew back, I got a call from Jerry. After his commission was taken out I would receive $16,560.00 for my idea. It wasn't lost on me that the amount covered what my week with Kristal had cost and then some.

~~***~~

But the fantasy had one more act to play. It was two months after my fantasy week had taken place. I was fixing dinner when the phone rang. My hands were busy so I pushed the button that put the phone on speaker.

"Hello?"

"Hi sweetie, miss me?"

"You know I do."

"Enough to want to see me again?"

"What do you have in mind?"

"An all-expense paid week in Hollywood and a week's work in the entertainment industry."

"Go on."

"You know what a fluffer is in my business?"

"She's the girl who gets the guys ready to perform, right?"

"Right. I need a fluffer sweetie. Someone to warm me up and get me ready to take on the male star of my next video. I thought of you sweetie. Would you like the job?"

"I'm sure that he would love the job," Joan said, "But I've got him back and I intend to keep him so thank you, but no thank you," and she pushed the button to disconnect.

"That was rude. Shouldn't you have let me do my own talking?"

"No way lover. No way could I trust you to say no to that sexpot. You are mine and I'll do whatever I have to do to keep you to myself."

"A bit possessive are we?"

"Damned straight lover, damned straight."

The End

Here is a sample from another story you may enjoy:

JUST PLAIN BOB

OPEN MIKE
NIGHT
A LANDING STRIP STORY

I came into the bar and when my eyes adjusted to the light, I looked toward the table in the back corner and saw what I expected to see. She was there with seven of her co-workers. Not counting her, there were three females and four males. She had always maintained that there was no dating going on in the group and that all they were were co-workers stopping for a few drinks after work, but I knew better. I'd seen too many of them leave in pairs for me to believe that story and after seeing it too many times, I wasn't ready to believe that she wasn't doing the same thing.

I headed over and took a seat at the bar with my back to the table, but I was able to see them in the mirror behind the bar. Melody came up and set a Pabst Blue Ribbon down in front of me as she said:

"Back to do it again, I see."

"Yep."

"I'll never understand why."

"Of course, you do. Joe doesn't make me pay for my drinks and doing it keeps me off the streets and out of trouble."

"You probably already noticed that she's here."

"Yep. I saw her back there with her group."

"Why does she keep coming in?"

"Her sister says that she does it so that when I see her, I'll be reminded of what I'm missing by not going back home to her. What she apparently doesn't realize is that every time I see her with that group, I'm reminded of why I'm no longer with her."

Just then, Joe Lambert, the owner of the Landing Strip Lounge, stepped up on the platform that the bands used on Fridays and Saturdays and spoke into the microphone.

"Good evening ladies and gentlemen and welcome to open mike night at The Strip. It is good to see such a large turnout for our would be stars so without further ado, I'll turn the microphone over to our home grown master of ceremonies, Bobby Denton."

I took the stage and Joe handed me the mike. "Good evening and welcome to what I expect to be a good night here at The Strip. We have some pretty good talent here for you tonight and as always, anyone who wants to give it a try only needs to walk up and tell me and we will give you your shot.

"For those of you who are new to this, the way it works is that Joe picks a topic and our performers take Joe's topic and ad-lib their performances. Tonight's topic is President Obama's health care plan. Our performers are allowed to go off topic, but only if they have a blond joke to tell and tradition has it that I start off the show with a blond joke in honor of my wife who is blond and who detests blond jokes.

"There was this blond who married a Catholic. On their honeymoon, the blond bride slipped into a sexy nightie and, with great anticipation, crawled into bed only to find that her new Catholic husband had settled down on the couch. When she asked him why he was apparently not going to make love to her he replied:

"It's Lent."

"In tears she sobbed. 'Well that is the most ridiculous thing I've ever heard. Who did you lend it to and for how long?'"

As I finished the joke, I looked at the table where Bree was sitting and the look on her face made me smile.

"Having touched on Catholics, I'll bring up one Catholic's alternative to Obama's health care plan. A man suffered a serious heart attack while shopping in a store. The store clerks called 911 when they saw him collapse on the floor. The paramedics rushed the man to the nearest hospital where he had emergency open-heart bypass surgery.

"He awakened from the surgery to find himself in the care of the nuns at the Catholic hospital he had been taken to. A nun was seated at his bedside holding a pen and a clipboard with several forms on it. She asked him how he was going to pay for his treatment.

"Do you have insurance?" she asked.

The man relied in a raspy voice, "Ain't got no health insurance."

The nun asked, "Do you have money in the bank?"

The man replied, "Ain't got no money in the bank."

"Do you have a relative who can help you with the payments?" she asked the irritated nun.

The man said, "I only have a spinster sister and she is a nun."

The nun became agitated and loudly announced, "Nuns are not spinsters! Nuns are married to God!"

The man replied, "Perfect. Send the bill to my brother in law."

If you enjoyed this sample then look for **Open Mike Night – A Landing Strip Story.**

Also by this Author:

The Prodigal Family: The Abbotts

Watching My Shared Wife

The Waitress and the Runaway Husband

Baiting Mr. Little

Too Hot for Henry

Chuck's Fantasy

Wife Sharing and Other Adventures

The Redhead's Desires

Rescued at Riley's

From the Author

If you enjoyed any of my books then please share the love and promote my books in Amazon.

If you write me a review and send me an email I will send you a free book, or many.
(Just know that these emails are filtered by my publisher.)

Good news is always welcome.

One Last Thing, For Kindle Readers...

When you turn the page, Kindle will give you the opportunity to rate this book and share your thoughts on Facebook and Twitter. If you enjoyed my writings, would you please take a few seconds to let your friends know about it? Because... when they enjoy they will be grateful to you and so will I.

Thank You!

An Open Letter from Just Plain Bob

A message for those who like my stories, those who hate my stories, those who are indifferent and those who have yet to make up their minds.

I have often stated that I really don't care what others think about my stories, that I write for my own enjoyment and then I offer to share. If you like my stories fine and if you don't, also fine since I have already satisfied my target audience - me!

It is human nature to strive to get better. If you take up bowling your first games are going low scoring, but you will work and practice to get better and as your average climbs you may forget the game where you had three gutter balls and shot an eighty-six, but that game is still there in your past.

Your first time on the golf course you shot an eighty on the front nine, but did you settle for that being your game or did you work to improve? You may eventually get a three handicap, but that nine hole eighty is still there as part of your past.

When you hired in at your job did you say, "Cool, I got it made" and do nothing more than what you barely had to do or did you go to work thinking that, "Someday I'm going to be running this place." You might never climb that high, but human nature says that you are going to at least try.

It is the same with authors who write stories and post them on sites like Literotica. Their first stories might not be all that good, but comments and feedback along with a desire to get better drive them toward putting out a better product or to at least try.

I'm no different. My first stories might not have been all that great, but they are still there on the hard drive. I like cheating wife stories and five years ago I found my first adult site that catered to cheating wife stories. It was a pay site, but it had a policy of giving a free lifetime membership to anyone who submitted five stories to the site. How hard can that be I said to myself as I sat down and fired up the word processor and went to work.

I sent my five stories in and sat back to enjoy my free membership and a funny thing happened. I started getting feedback, most of it positive, and I became hooked. I started cranking out more stories. The site I was sending my stories to had seven categories:

Bisexual
Cream Pie
Groups

I Watch
Gang Bang
Racial
SM/BD

I know nothing about bisexual or SM/BD and I had no interest in Groups so all the stories I wrote I tailored for the four remaining categories:

Cream Pie
I Watch
Gang Bang
Racial.

I turned out eight stories a month, two for each category, which means that after five years I have over 120 stories in each of those categories and they are all still on the hard drive.

A year ago I received an email asking me why I never posted stories on Literotica. The answer? I didn't know about Lit. I pulled it up, liked what I saw, and started sending in stories to it. All new stories? No, not hardly, not with over 400 stories sitting on the hard drive. Maybe one new story for each fifteen or so old ones. The newer ones are better, at least I think they are and I have received some feedback that leads me to believe that others think so too, and I will continue to write new ones.

But I am still going to recycle what is on the hard drive, stories that were written specifically to fit the four categories. That means that those of you who hate cream pie stories still have eighty or so to look forward to. Ditto for those who call me a racist; you will get another seventy or so interracial stories.

Those who hate wimps will only see about fifty more of those because the stories I sent to the I Watch category were split 50/50 between what some call wimps and some call "real men." Why the 50/50 split? It came from listening to the readers. I would get feedback asking me why all the men in my stories were hard asses. "In real life men are more forgiving, especially if it is the first indiscretion." So I would write stories with forgiving husbands and boyfriends and then the next batch of feedback would say, "Why are all your husbands spineless wimps" and I'd write stories that went back the other way.

Eventually I came to realize that I was wasting my time - there was no way I could write a story that would satisfy everybody and that is when I adopted my philosophy of writing for my own enjoyment and then offering to share.

As far as the gangbang stories? Well, what can I say? Gangbangs are gangbangs and there are still eighty or so of them to go.

The bottom line is that Literotica readers are going to see more of my old stories than my new ones. If I'm still around three or four years from now it will probably go the other way, more new than old.

I feel the need to respond to some of the comments and emails I have received. By far the largest percentage comes from people who say, "You are an asshole because all women are not whores and sluts and that's all you make them out to be."

Next most common is, "You must really hate women you sick fuck."

"You must be a wimp because all the men in your stories are wimps" is up there in the top ten along with, "Why don't you give it a rest and go crawl off in a hole somewhere."

There is a lot more, but I'm only going to address those four and in reverse order.

I won't stop and go crawl in a hole because I am enjoying the hell out of what I am doing and remember what I said, I am doing this for MY OWN ENJOYMENT and then I offer to share. Some obviously like my sharing with them and so I will continue to do so. No one is holding a gun to a reader's head and telling them they must click on a Just Plain Bob story or die. It is a conscious choice on the reader's part to move that mouse and click on that story.

When a man finds out he has a cheating wife or girlfriend there are only a limited number of ways he can handle it. If he loves her he can forgive, try to forget and try to hold on and somehow make things work. He can turn his back on her, walk away and get on with his life. The third option is to take revenge.

According to a good portion of those who send me feedback the first and second options are proof that the men are wimps. If the man takes the third option he is still considered a wimp if he doesn't do some sort of physical damage to the woman and her lover. These readers believe that the only way not to be a wimp is to kill, maim and destroy everything in sight. Doing that however, will invariably get the man throw in jail and that is why it so rarely happens in real life.

In real life most revenge takes place in the man's head when he says to himself, "I should have _____ (fill in the blank) the fucking cunt!" I know this because I have been there and done that (see The Dark Trilogy). In my stories I try to mirror real life so kill, maim and destroy are going to be for the most part absent. Outside of some fisticuffs there will be very little physical violence in my stories. Most of my husbands are going to do what I did, what several of my friends and others that I know have done, forgive, or walk away. If this makes them wimps and me a wimp for writing the story that way, so be it.

Next is the "I must hate all women." Nothing could be farther from the truth. I love women. I lust after women. I even like whores and sluts. I have been married four times, engaged two other times (that did not end in marriage) and I have always had girlfriends between marriages. My philosophy is that women were put on this earth for me to enjoy and I'm not talking just sexually. I could sit at the mall (and have) for hours and just girl watch.

The engagements, girlfriends and three of the four marriages bring me to the #1 anti JPB comment on the list.

"You are an asshole because all women aren't whores and sluts."

Well dear reader, you can not prove that by me! I will say up front that I KNOW all women aren't whores and sluts, BUT the majority of the women in my life were. My mother ran around on my father for years while he was driving a truck for a living. My Aunt Margaret cheated regularly on my Uncle Bill, as did my Aunt Mildred on my Uncle Paul. My Aunt Betty fucked around on my Uncle Bob for years and finally left him for his brother, my Uncle Wendell. Uncle Wendell in turn caught her on her knees at his company Christmas party giving Season's Greetings to his boss.

My sister is three times divorced and each divorce came about when the then current husband caught her out spreading pollen. Both of the engagements I mentioned ended when I found out that I was not the one and only and a lot of the girls I dated between marriages never made it to engagement status for the same reason.

And that brings me to my three ex-wives. The first one, Helen (I believe I commented on her in the intro to The Dark Trilogy) had seven different lovers before I found out what was going on. I was living proof that love is blind. Ditto with my second wife. She had a secret life that she hid from me and when I found out about her brother, his friends and the gangbangs she was history.

My third marriage ended in divorce because of a different kind of cheating (and I can just imagine the outrage I am going to get over this) - she cheated on me with an idea. I was away from home on business, she was lonely, a couple of Jehovah's Witnesses knocked on the door and my wife, with nothing better to do invited them in. When I came home from my trip I found out that she had found God. On a scale that runs from TRUE BELIEVER on one end to ATHEIST on the other you will find me just to the right of AGNOSTIC and since I would not allow myself to be SAVED the marriage eventually died.

So yes, I write about sluts and whores because as everyone knows, you tend to write about the things you know. And I do like sluts and whores, just not the ones that lie to me and cheat on me.

So be forewarned - if you click on a Just Plain Bob story you will be getting sluts, whores and husbands who do not kill, maim and destroy. There are other things you will rarely find in a Just Plain Bob story. Even though I try to mirror real life my stories all take place in StoryLand. In StoryLand STDs and unwanted pregnancies do not exist unless the author feels like they may add something to the story. Bad things do not happen in StoryLand unless the author so wills it and no amount of "You should have..." in comments and feedback will change a story already posted.

Lastly, I will touch on a truth. None of what I have written here means shit because the same readers will still read the same stories that they profess to hate and make the same comments they have always made. Knowing this, I will deliberately post stories that will have them frothing at the mouth.

It is the least I can do for an adoring public.

Thank you!

Just Plain Bob
justplainbob@awesomeauthors.org